For Daisy Mae

Text and illustrations copyright © 2018 by Jeff Mack
All rights reserved.

Published by Two Lions, New York
www.apub.com

Amazon, the Amazon logo, and Two Lions are trademarks of Amazon.com, Inc.,
or its affiliates.

ISBN-13 9781503902923
ISBN-10 1503902927

The illustrations are rendered in digital media
Book design by Tanya Ross-Hughes

Printed in China
First Edition
10 9 8 7 6 5 4 3 2 1

JEFF MACK

two lions

Every night, it's the same old story.

Then, in the morning, something is always just a little weird.

HOW DID YOU GET UP THERE?

So here's what I want to know:

Do they paint?

Do they draw?

So one night,
I listened.

I thought I heard voices.

But I couldn't believe what I saw . . .

Mom? Dad? Duck?
They were party animals!

They ate a ton of snacks!

Then they rocked the house.

. . . then they fell . . .

. . . where they slept.

In the morning, the house was so quiet,
I thought it must have been a dream.

Then again, maybe it wasn't.

Either way,
I know one thing for sure . . .

I can't wait to grow up.